EDDIE GOES TO SCHOOL

CAROLINA HUGGARE

ILLUSTRATIONS CAMILA DE GODOY
ADAPTATION MONICA MURPHY

SHE IS RESPONSIBLE FOR
MAKING IT THAT PRETTY!

GRAPHIC DESIGN AND LAYOUT   MARCELLA PAVANI

SHE CORRECTED THE TEXT
AND SET UP THE BOOK.

REVISON   NATHALIA FERRAREZI

PLANNING   ALINE GONGORA → SHE PARTICIPATED IN THE ENTIRE BOOK
PLANNING PROCESS.

ILLUSTRATIONS   CAMILA DE GODOY

SHE DID ALL OF THESE WONDERFUL DRAWINGS! ←

TRANSLATION   MONICA MURPHY → SHE TRANSLATED CAROL'S STORY.

PRODUCED IN BRAZIL → COUNTRY WHERE THE BOOK WAS PRODUCED.

Index card prepared by
Liliane Castro – Librarian CRB-8/6748

THE INDEX CARD SHEET HAS THE
NECESSARY INFORMATION TO IDENTIFY AND
TO LOCATE A BOOK IN A LIBRARY.

H891e   Huggare, Carolina
Eddie Goes to School / Carolina Huggare ; illustrations Camila de Godoy ;
adaptation Monica Murphy –
1st ed. – São Paulo: Ma Petite Amélie, 2021.
24 p. : il.

Original title: Dudu vai a escola
ISBN 978-65-992178-5-. ⟶ ISBN IS AN IDENTIFICATION SYSTEM USING NUMBERS TO CLASSIFY BOOKS

1. Children's literature 2. Autism spectrum disorder 3. Inclusion
I. Godoy, Camila de. II. Subject.

CDD: 028.5
CDU: 82-93

EDDIE GOES TO SCHOOL IS BOOK N. 3 OF "MA PETITE AMÉLIE"
WHEN IT IS TIME, JUMP WITHOUT HESITATING.
BE AN INDEPENDENT AUTHOR. PUBLISH WITH AMÉLIE.
SEND YOUR ORIGINAL FOR ANALYSIS: PLANEJAMENTO@AMELIEEDITORIAL.COM.
WWW.AMELIEEDITORIAL.COM

To Lars and Alice, my heroes,
with all my love.

Eddie goes to school.

Eddie wants mommy to stay.

He does not like loud noises...

and sometimes he does not want to play.

But Eddie likes learning,

and snack-time,

and running.

Some days he likes to swing and slide.
Some days he feels overwhelmed and
wants to hide.

Is Eddie different?

Sometimes he feels happy,
sometimes he feels blue.

Eddie is one of a kind, just like you.

Made in the USA
Columbia, SC
14 July 2021

41855609R00015